WHY DID THE FARMER CROSS THE ROAD?

Written by Brooke Herter James

Illustrated by Mike Herrod

For Dave
—B.H.J.

To my little men, Linus and Max.
—M.H.

The illustrations in this book were rendered in pen and ink with watercolor.

Text Copyright © 2017 Brooke Herter James
Illustration Copyright © 2017 Mike Herrod
Design Copyright @ 2017 Sleeping Bear Press

Sleeping Bear Press
2395 South Huron Parkway, Suite 200
Ann Arbor, MI 48104
www.sleepingbearpress.com

Printed and bound in China.

10 9 8 7 6 5 4 3 2 1

Library of Congress Cataloging-in-Publication Data

Names: James, Brooke Herter, author. | Herrod, Mike, illustrator.
Title: Why did the farmer cross the road? / written by Brooke Herter James ; illustrated by Mike Herrod.
Description: Ann Arbor, MI : Sleeping Bear Press, [2017] | Summary: While Donkey tries to convince Farmer that all the other animals have left the farm, chickens, goats, and even a cow are enjoying rides and contests at a fair.
Identifiers: LCCN 2016026768 | ISBN 9781585369638
Subjects: | CYAC: Domestic animals—Fiction. | Fairs—Fiction. | Farmers—Fiction. | Humorous stories.
Classification: LCC PZ7.1.J3848 Why 2017 | DDC [E]—dc23
LC record available at https://lccn.loc.gov/2016026768

It's early, Donkey.

Yes, Sir. But this is urgent! The pigs are escaping!

Escaping?

They're halfway down Sherman Avenue, headed towards town!

Not possible, Donkey. Go back to bed.

I know you're out there, Donkey. I can hear you breathing.

It's just that, well, the cow is on her way, too.

Let me guess. To town? By herself?

No, Sir. She's following the sheep.

And the chickens??? To town as well?

Yes, Sir. Flown the coop.

So that leaves the goats and you. Is that right, Donkey?

Actually, just me, Sir.

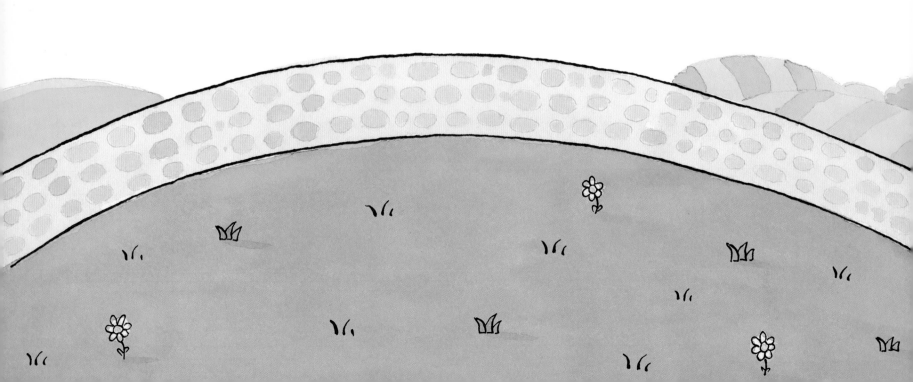

Is this some kind of **JOKE**, Donkey? Is there something going on in town that I should know about??

This, Sir.

Well, son of a gun. I **KNEW** I heard a merry-go-round. It's just a **FAIR**, Donkey. What's the worst that could happen?!

Really, Sir?

Oh, all right, Donkey. Meet me at the truck. We'll go get them.

Would you be all right with this, Sir? It's just that the truck ...

JUST DRIVE, DONKEY. If we're ever going to get there, it **MIGHT** be a good idea to get there before the Pie Eating Contest begins ...

Oh dear.

Well, let's load 'em up, Donkey, and go home.

Donkey, I'm not **MAD** at you or anything,
but just exactly how did all this happen?

I believe you left the barn door open, Sir.